Rocks in My Pockets

The Tales and Essays of Ryan James Loyd

Ryan Loyd

PublishAmerica
Baltimore

© 2004 by Ryan James Loyd.
All rights reserved. No part of this book may be reproduced, stored in a retrieval system or transmitted in any form or by any means without the prior written permission of the publishers, except by a reviewer who may quote brief passages in a review to be printed in a newspaper, magazine or journal.

First printing

ISBN: 1-4137-4452-4
PUBLISHED BY PUBLISHAMERICA, LLLP
www.publishamerica.com
Baltimore

Printed in the United States of America

A Quandary of Quagmires

As I inched out onto the log, it responded with an ominous crunching sound, my boot-heels sinking into the long deadwood. I raised an eyebrow in query, and squinted across the not-close-enough-to-jump-it expanse of watery mire. The glare of the afternoon sun, even through the cover of weeds, made me sorry I had neglected to follow that most crucial rule of proper adventuring—never forget your hat.

With a sigh, I eyed the seemingly innocuous strip of water, being only four inches deep it seemed I would only become minorly wet if my bridge were to collapse in mid crossing, but I knew just by looking that the mud entombed in those shallow depths was none other than sneaky, God awful, hip deep, foul smellin' swamp muck—and having made *that* particular error more than once in my early days of adventuring, I was not at all enthusiastic about reliving the experience. For when your boots fill with water, and that slimy mud begins its inevitable advance past the waistband of your underwear, there is nothing quite so disconcerting in this world as the small, squirming realization that you are not alone in your pants.

I gave the log a stomp and a wiggle. The center still seemed solid enough, so with a shrug and a grin I began to traverse my treacherous path. Step one and two were just fine, and by step three I even began to get a little cocky.

"No Problem," I said to myself. I should have known better, of course, for step number four brought the slightest hint of a creaking through the soles of my boots, and step number five began that terrible, slow sag of rotten logs. I froze. The log held. All was good. Except for the fact that I was now stuck, precariously balanced over a fell-looking bog, inhabited by a thousand-thousand small icky things that would probably not be pleased to make my acquaintance—nor I theirs for that matter, and the structural integrity of my bridge was now questionable at best.

What to do? I could go back the way I came and find another route, but if I had wanted to do that, I would've in the first place. So steeling myself against a soggy, muck-covered fate I took step number six. There was a *Crack*, and I cursed as the log jolted an inch or two lower. And then the cautious seventh step, which set into motion an unsalvageable roll. Branches rose from the water like skeletal hands trailing black moss to sweep me into the depths of nameless horrors below. With a yelp and a wild leap I careened from the log to the scant shore, and with great alarm I realized that I could not stop on my emergency runway and would inevitably plough headfirst into the swamp, unless I could come up with and execute some amazing escape in the next half second!

The poor little sweet gum tree never saw it coming. It was seized by savage, desperate hands and nearly yanked from the earth as I came to an abrupt stop, boot-heels dug into the mossy ground and suspended at a most alarming angle out over the water. My heart thundered in my ears as the momentum carried me in a short arc ending when I collided soundly with a large oak tree. Yeah, it hurt. But at least I escaped the mire…

Words

"Why do you always use them big words?"
They would demand
as if words of four or five letters
were some infectious disease
with which I might corrupt them.
I would just shrug and go hide in some corner,
away from their accusing glares
to ponder which word
had carried me yet again
beyond the unspoken boundaries
of acceptable third grade vocabulary.
Most of them, I would realize with a bewildered sigh.
Further reinforcing my long held belief
that school was just a shorter word
for Purgatory.

Duke the Boat-dog

That winter proved to be quite mild, all in all, but the nights were still quite chill. It was on one such chilly night that dear ol' Dad had a plan.

"C'mon, boy, we're gonna teach Duke how to be a boat-dog…" he said to me after dinner.

For a moment I thought he was kidding, for I was fairly certain that stickin' a hundred and eighty pound Great Dane in a canoe in the middle of winter would be an ill-fated venture indeed. With a sinking feeling I realized that Dad was already making preparations to embark and was not kidding in the slightest .

"Um… Dad? Uh… You sure this is a good idea?" I asked with a grimace that I hoped would convey my trepidations on the matter.

"Sure! Why wouldn't it be?" said Dad cheerfully. I just shook my head and sighed as Dad hollered for Duke. It had been quite some time since Dad had a proper boat-dog.

Who knows, I thought to myself, *maybe he can pull it off…* But a little voice in the back of my head replied, *When you hit that water…*

Mother stuck her head out the kitchen door. "You're not planning to take Duke in the boat are you?"

Her tone plainly indicating what she thought of the idea.

"Yep," said Dad, undaunted by her skepticism.

"That's not too smart if you ask me," said Mother, "putting a dog that big in a canoe is just plain foolish."

"Nah," Dad replied, "we can manage it!"

I knew, of course, that Mother was right as usual, but Dad's enthusiasm got the better of me. Mother went back inside, disgusted by our wanton ignorance, shaking her head and muttering something it's probably better I couldn't make out, leaving us to our endeavor.

Duke had arrived and was sniffing the boat with interest.

"Hup!" said Dad, patting the side of the boat.

Duke just looked at him with his big dopey Great Dane grin.

"Hup!" said Dad again, this time snapping his fingers.

Duke plopped down on his massive haunches. Dad looked perplexed.

"Hey, Dad? I don't think he knows *Hup*..." I said. Which was fine by me of course, for if Duke couldn't figure out how to get in the boat, we wouldn't wind up in the drink.

"He'll learn... Why don't you hop out and give him a little assistance?" Translation: pick him up and put him in the boat.

With a groan I stepped out onto the soggy bank. Duke, for some unfathomable reason, was so excited to have me back on land with him that he almost bounded me right into the lake. But soon enough I had him calmed down and managed with great effort and numerous curses to heave the front half of his smelly bulk into the canoe (all the while Dad saying, Hup! Hup! for all the good that did.)

Duke, having at long last achieved that most mysterious aluminum craft, lolled his great tongue in doggish pride. The only problem was he, thinking he was in the boat, refused to budge another inch and no amount of coaxing could convince him otherwise. Dad could offer no assistance, for he was keeping the canoe on the shore, so it was up to me to oversee the loading of Duke's latter half..

After a harrowing few seconds and several more curses, we were off the shore, Dad paddling merrily along, Duke in the middle somewhere between joyous and making a jump for it, and me fending off Duke's soggy bludgeon of a tail.

"Y'see?" Dad grinned, "I told you it'd be no problem."

I didn't share his optimism, for with all the new and interesting smells that needed investigating on either side of the boat, Duke's wobbling lurches and quaking legs made keeping the boat upright somewhat of a chore, not to mention the relentless assault of that damned tail. However, by this point I was resigned. I was certain that at any moment our wildly rocking craft would reach that terminal pivot which would dump Captain and crew into the dark frigid depths below, but my father, The Captain, skillfully kept our small craft afloat, even through the ordeal of Duke deciding he wanted to face the other way. After my heart slowed down, finally relieved of that weapon-like tail, I was able to actually enjoy the trip. All was silent, save for the sound of paddles swirling through the water and the echoes of the dog bumping on the sides of the boat. The stars shined through the blackness in all their winter brilliance, and I began to relax. We were approaching the far shore where the geese were languidly paddling undaunted by the cold, when Duke, deciding he needed to go ashore, leaped from the boat with a great splash. The canoe lurched dramatically and I was sure that was it, but Dad had matters well in hand and righted us quick as a flash. I felt as if a great weight had been lifted. We were dry (mostly), and were no longer in danger of being capsized by a giant dog who had no business in a canoe in the first place. Things were good.

We cruised along the shore, stopping several times at Dad's insistence to try to get Duke back in the boat. But no matter how many times Dad said, "Hup!" Duke would only hang his head over the side and grin. "Why don't you..." Dad began.

"Oooh no," I cut him off, "now he's soakin' wet, if you want him in here with us, you pick him up."

Dad declined. As we headed back home, Duke was content to

run along the levee and sniff things.

I breathed a long awaited sigh of relief as the nose of the boat bumped the shore.

"Wow, I can't believe we managed to pull that off!" I laughed. "I thought we'd wind up in the lake for sure!"

"See? What'd I tell you?" said Dad, as he began to rise in order to pull the boat ashore.

There was a sound not unlike a horse as Duke came careening out of the darkness, enraptured by our return to land, and that big, muddy, weapon-like tail caught Dad square across the eyes. As Dad tumbled with a yelp grasping blindly for balance, his hands found the side of the boat, whereupon he was transformed from The Captain into the perfect lever. I found myself airborne, ejected from my happy existence as first mate, demoted to the freezing cold, soaking wet position of man overboard. Curses upon curses I flung across the lake to echo through the winter night as I waded, shivering in the waist deep water, collecting lost cargo. When I squished my dripping way back to land Dad was overcome with mirth. He thought it was funny as hell. Apparently Duke did as well, for he danced around with a doggish approximation of a hearty guffaw.

Mother was not at all surprised to find us soaked to the bone, and although she didn't say it, the *I told you so's* were writ clear across her brow.

As we eased our frozen forms into the hot tub Dad remarked that we should probably wait till it got a little warmer before we tried again. I just grumbled through my chattering teeth and shook my head. Unfortunately for Duke, the not-quite-Boat-dog, he has yet to set foot in another boat. I for one would like to keep it that way.

Pockets

    I always dread going through the metal detectors at the airport, or any other place they make you empty out your pockets before proceeding. It's not that I generally carry about anything embarrassing or that I shouldn't have, it's just always such a pain to reload everything where it goes. I carry all the standard pocket stuff, of course—keys, wallet, checkbook and spare change, but then I've got the ever present pocketknife, an old leaky zippo, several assorted lucky rocks that I give to people who need them, one of those little pocket tools with the pliers and such, an ancient skeleton key on a leather thong that may or may not fit some lock somewhere in the world, a silver dollar from 1879 that my great, great grandfather carried, a cheap little lighter in case my zippo conks out, a notebook and a pen (for I am a writer, after all, and inspiration can strike at any given moment), peppermints of some form or another (though I do hate those cheap chewy ones), a small leather bag full of tiny crystals—just because—and all that is just if I'm traveling light.
    At any given time I could also have nails, string, bones, more knives, bits of chain, strange little boxes, fur, feathers, flowers, shells, or dirt, and on very rare occasions—something living. People always grant me odd stares as I deposit my treasures in the little bowls they give you (I usually overflow two of 'em), and sometimes they ask in a bewildered voice, "Why do you need all this stuff?" I fix them with an odd look and in most serious tones reply, "Just in case…"

Meeting Him

Her boyfriend towered over me by a whole foot, and the police light quivering in his hand was
obviously intended for my skull. (Not that I could really blame him for being upset, I mean, I was there to usurp his comfortable boyfriend position.)
There was an instant of indecision, where my mind reeled with possibilities of action. My warrior
nature screamed at me to whack him soundly and not stop till he quit twitching; however, that was quickly dismissed as excessive and stupid. I decided to fight fire with water as it were, and strode forward with a grin (and a big stick behind my back, I mean c'mon, I'm not stupid). I extended my hand in my friendliest greeting.

"Nice to meet you," I said, as if I had been planning all along to run into him in this very spot. The spasm of conflicting emotions that played across his visage was priceless to behold, and I suppressed   a giggle of triumph as he shook my hand with a resigned sort of sigh. I suppose he was simply
unprepared to deal with an armed and friendly individual, who seemed not the least bit concerned
by his size, armament, or station.

Of course, then he took her away, and left me standing alone in the chill Utah night, locked out of the house… In retrospect, I shoulda whacked him.

Arrrr! Boo-ty!

And so it was one fine summer day we set off in search of diamonds. Reason and logic told us in no uncertain terms that our venture to Murfrees Borough would, of course, come to naught, but before too many miles were behind us we had forgotten all about reason or logic and were soon lost in dreams of buried treasure and how we should divvy up our booty and make our mark upon the world as wealthy men.

The journey was a long one, and I must admit that we were lost more than once in the twisting maze that is Hot Springs and the small towns thereabout, but after two or three stops for directions we finally managed to lay in our proper course and arrived at our destination. After a cursory glance at the samples in the front office to discern exactly what it was we were looking for, we headed to the fabled Crater of Diamonds.

Now, just what I imagined a Crater of Diamonds to look like I'm not exactly sure, but a large ploughed field of dirt wasn't it. It occurred to us, as we poked around the slick ashen soil, that it wasn't going to be quite as easy as we had first surmised. And when we noticed a man shoulder deep in a great pit, covered in mud and furiously wielding a shovel, the reason and logic—which we had so conveniently left on the roadside—finally caught up with us, and our dreams of giant glimmering gemstones erupting from the earth suddenly faded 'neath the wrath of the merciless sun. So our spirits somewhat dampened, we turned our heels toward home, and our thoughts to more productive adventures. I hear there's a place in the Ozarks where you can still pan for gold…

And now an excerpt from the backwoods Play-Actin' Troup's rendition of Macbeth

Wing of bat, barf of gnat, pecker of a big black cat,
Swamp muck from down in yonder hole,
Stirred up with cow pies in a bowl,
Moonshine from my grandpappy's still,
Red buckeye found on yonder hill
When I got drunk up there last year,
Possum snot, and hound dawg's ear.
Bladder of a rabid skunk,
Twelve black pellets of used buck shot
An' a few deer parts, just startin' to rot,
Add at the end a spit of chew,
To the stuff that's in our witchy brew
Bubble, bubble, big black pot,
Don't you touch it,
The damn thang's hot!

Dirt Dauber

The dirt dauber's bluish hue was lost in the failing light of day, rendering the insect black as jet. I watched as she flew to and fro, a filmy substance the color of dark amber clutched in her mandibles, completely obscuring her vision. She crashed into the screen, backed up, and did it again. Deciding that this approach wasn't accomplishing much, she flew in a large circle and collided with the screen a third time. Fortunately for the dirt dauber, she managed to cling with one foot so as to avoid being bounced airborne once again.

By this time the little insect had my undivided attention. I was extremely curious, for as she crawled madly around the screen in a seemingly vain attempt to dislodge her odd burden I began to wonder if she had it, or it had her; but as she continued 'round and 'round the screen, it seemed that she was looking for just the right spot. Finally she found it. She stopped, took a step over, and dropped her load—which I had by now realized was an old larval casing from a previously owned dirt dauber nest.

She paused to clean her antennae and flew off. I didn't think anything else of it and so returned my attention to sipping my coffee and gazing off into the hills. That is, until she returned a moment or two later, back to the same routine of flying, crashing, crawling, dropping, and cleaning, and then she was off again. This time I watched as she flew, in long circles, the length of the porch, ramming into every rafter along the way, until finally on her third pass she came to rest on the large abandoned nest of carefully packed mud that was her palace (located a mere foot and a half to the right of her drop zone). It was an impressive nest, and old—home to untold generations of dirt daubers. It boasted at least fifteen brood dens, one of which she promptly disappeared into, only to emerge a second later bearing another piece of amber larval casing. She took to the air to crash once more, and cling once more, and search, and drop, and clean.

I had seen enough. My coffee was gone, it was hot out there on the porch, I didn't think I'd miss much after my departure, and I knew the dirt dauber would continue her immaculate cleansing whether I observed or not.

How much pee on a tree
does it take to say
Mine!
Determined little dog?
Once I would think
should suffice.
O' scrabble and sniff
and scrabble and pee
Anymore piss shall
kill that tree
It's your's I swear,
You can have it
says me!
Just cease your assault
on the poor little tree.
Thy bladder is huge
I'll admit I'm impressed,
But you're down to just dribbles
so do give it a rest.
Your master is waiting
and wanting away,
There's more trees in the forest
to bring under sway.
Pee no more, little dog
I beseech, no! I Pray!
And thus stated, he bounded
quite happ'ly away…

The Incident With the Lucky Rock

Perhaps it was the two double cappuccinos, or, then again, perhaps it was fear that set my form to quaking so that I was certain I looked like a Chihuahua who desperately needed to pee.

Each timid step brought me ever closer to an encounter with the young lady in the shadowed corner. Each step brought a fresh wave of doubt crashing about my ears and sent my heart careening against my ribcage. I desperately wished that she would raise her head from whatever thoughts she put to pen and take note of my approach. At the same moment, I desperately hoped that she wouldn't.

The black stone, almost round and polished marble smooth through adventuresome miles spent riding in my pocket, granted me some measure of comfort as it rested in my palm, which I was not at all pleased to note had grown quite damp in that inexplicably long expanse of a mere twenty feet. Suddenly and most unexpectedly I found myself at her small table, and she, being quite engrossed in her writing, took no notice.

"Pardon me," I was going to say, "might I join you for a moment?"

What I was going to say after that I really wasn't sure, but if I could just manage that first part, everything would be Okay.

So, steeling myself with a deep breath, I stepped forward that last fateful step.

"Pardon me," I said.

At this point she was supposed to look up and take note of my somewhat traumatized presence. In retrospect, perhaps I spoke a little too softly, for her pen continued its sojourn across the page, and as the eons ticked by I began to feel rather foolish.

After what must have been at least three and a half seconds—like an actor whose cue has been skipped by a page and a half, I covered. I nonchalantly exited stage left through a conveniently located door that led to the bathrooms. I stood in the hallway cursing myself for my cowardice and whacked myself soundly on the head, which of course merely added injury to insult, and so I made my way to the men's room rubbing my sore brow.

The mirror delivered a stern lecture on the particulars of self confidence and ordered me back to my quest. My courage, though wounded, was not mortally so, but it couldn't hold for long. With an air of definite purpose, I strode to the door but my hand faltered upon the knob, and my purposeful air was banished as surely as cold iron dispels a Faerie glamour.

I should just admit that I'm a chicken and go sit down, forget about the whole thing, I thought.

I almost jumped out of my skin as my mother's voice rang through my head like a clarion: "Just go and do it already!"

Though I failed to make it out of my skin, I did jump enough that the door popped open, spilling garish florescent light from the hall all over her nice shadowy table. She didn't look terribly pleased.

"Um… Excuse me," I stammered.

"Yes," she said—she didn't sound terribly pleased either.

All thoughts fled like sheep in a field, bleating wildly, so as not only to leave me thoughtless, but to prevent me from coming up with any new ones as well.

"Ah…" I fought the urge to bolt for my table and dive beneath the tablecloth in a fit of hysterics. "Here," I blurted out, thrusting the stone forward. "This is for you…"

She looked at me with an unfathomable expression.

"It's a lucky rock," I said lamely, expending the last ounce of confidence I had. I have no idea how she reacted, for I took to my heels without so much as a backward glance and fled back to my table, feeling like the world's biggest goofball.

The Things We Forget

The Barefoot times are upon us once again, and we shed our heavy boots and free ourselves of the hot, damp confines of sweaty socks to run free o'er the fresh green grass so cool and refreshing to tired toes… That's something along the lines of what I was thinking as I ran joyously through the yard, feeling free and happy in the warm sun. Then I encountered the domain of the sweetgum tree. The ground was littered all about with gumballs, their brittle phalanx of brown spikes just waiting to shred my poor feet softened by months of shoes. It was far too late to stop, and years of experience taught me that as sure as I put on the breaks I would inevitably stomp square on a patch of them and, being things that roll, I'd wind up flat on my back.

So I performed a wild and panicked hopscotch, bouncing from one clear spot to another in a vain attempt to reach the safety of the grass once more. I thought rather smugly that I had made it clear through, and grinned at my skill. Of course, one should never think that when running through a field of gumballs, barefoot, and I paid for my hubris with blood and curses as I hopped from one injured foot to the other, each hop landing me on yet another one. By the end of the summer, I will have forgotten all about this event, for by then I'll be able to run across broken glass without a second thought. But next year when this comes up again, I'll remember far too late, just as I always do.

T's Kitchen

Steam begins to condense on the door of the microwave oven hanging above the stove, as the scents of garlic and oregano fill the air. She wipes her brow between her rapid stirrings, leaving a streak of flour there. On anyone else it might have looked comical, but Mother can wear even smudges with style. Away to the refrigerator she whisks in a flash, and after much clanking of jars and rummaging of drawers, she returns once more to the stove of bubbling concoctions halfway done and becoming critical.

In measurements of this much, and that much, and five or six shakes (and another for good measure, for much of the herb missed the pot and now adorns the wall) she works her culinary magic, unhindered by teaspoons or other exact implements. By feel and by taste she knows when all is right.

She is master of her kitchen, this sorceress of spice, and not even the near loss of a fingertip will slow her down. She just snatches a paper towel with a curse and a hasty wrapping, and heedless of the blood spurting from her finger, she checks the pasta to see if it is yet al dente.

And amid the chaotic mess of the countertop, she draws forth a feast so wondrous t'would make a king weep

Then we sit at the table, to talk and to dine, to stuff ourselves silly on the immaculate dish till we can hardly move.

"Sorry for the throw-together dinner..." she says with a wrinkling of her brow.

And all I can do is shake my head with a confused sort of smile, for all the while I've been pitying the patrons of fine restaurants, the world over, for having to subsist on such poor fare.

Boiled Lobster, Anyone?

After the long day spent playing in the glorious Memorial Day sun, I found myself wishing that I had not scoffed at the proffered sunblock, for I both looked and felt rather like a boiled crustacean. It's yet another of those lessons that I always forget about during the long winter as my flesh wanes from its summer bronze back to Scot's Irish fishbelly tones.

But the sun is ever ruthless in its reminder, cooking me crispy as I play in blissful summer oblivion.

The worst thing about it was my ill-fated attempt at a shower, for though my hand assured me that the temperature was fine before I stepped in, the first brush of water across my shoulders sent me shrieking back out again, certain that I'd been scalded. So I adjusted the water and attempted it again. This time it was rather pleasant on my poor sunburn, but the rest of me was positively freezing, and in the attempt to remedy this unpleasantness I knocked the hot water handle a little too far and sent myself hissing and cursing out of the shower door once more. Finally I managed to attain a rather unhappy medium that only hurt a little, yet didn't set my teeth to chattering, that still managed to be terribly unpleasant due to its sickly tepid nature. Oh well, Another lesson driven home for the hundredth time—sunblock, you idiot, sunblock.

Words That Stay...

    Being a writer is not so simple a thing as it sounds. Well, that is to say, sometimes it's simplicity itself, and it's all you can do to keep hold of your pen as the words leap into existence unbidden and seemingly of their own accord, as if they were already there and the writer were merely their chosen means of making themselves known to the world.
    Other times it seems that the words turn timid and rather shy in nature. These must be carefully coaxed from the places that words hide and in the end, with some patience, they come along willingly enough and fall into place with relative ease, (though some of the most timid ones can take a good deal of searching and often push other hapless words to the fore in hopes that they won't be noticed).
    But then there are the days when the words just won't come, and no amount of coaxing, cajoling, or coffee can make them be. And thus the writer sits in idle purgatory, 'neath the weight of a furrowed brow—his pen tapping upon an open notebook with a rhythmic hollow thump that bores into his mind. The lines stretch across the bleached page like roads into a barren waste, and the mocking white glare of the all too empty spaces between stares back at him accusingly with near audible whispers of doom. The writer wracks his poor brain, willing his motionless pen to mar the abysmal expanse of page before him with some insight, some outpouring of wisdom, something, anything!! The writer knows that all it would take would be one word, one single word scribed in black ink, and his muse would be freed from her white walled

prison, to charge to his rescue with a whole army of words with which to smite the mocking page back into submission. But alas, the pen just hovers there, poised and waiting for a sign, a flash of inspiration that never seems to come…

Sitting half drunk
in the gruesomely 50s style diner,
I find that I truly
despise electric pink…

Dude

So, in lieu of my renowned fear of asking girls out, I decided to give the whole Internet dating thing a try. After a bit of searching I found a fair-looking free site and posted a profile, and sure enough I got a response within a few days. Well anyway, I emailed this person back and forth for a bit and they seemed rather nifty, though I refused to get my hopes up too high for this was the Internet after all, where anyone could be anyone and no one would be the wiser. We decided one night to meet for coffee, and I must admit I was rather nervous at the prospect, for it hit me then that this was on par with a blind date. When she finally arrived, something seemed a tad bit amiss. I mean, I do know girls who are six foot two, and I suppose girls who happen to be six foot two would be entitled to have a rather deep-ish voice. I shrugged it off and we went inside for our coffee. She was a very nice person and as it happened we had a delightful conversation, but I just couldn't get over the fact that something didn't seem quite right. Perhaps it had something to do with her large thick knuckles and distinctly unfeminine hands, or perhaps it was the squarish set of her jaw and heavy brow ridge that told me that I was probably buying coffee for a man in drag. When we finished our coffee I thanked this person for the company and went on my merry way, never to see them again. To each their own, of course, but that's having just a bit too much in common for me.

Sunday

Both of our alarms had been going off since seven o'clock that morning. The tones, already grating and dissonant enough on their own, clashed against each other like a banjo duel played upon a pair of unwilling geese. It must have seemed impossible for anyone to sleep through such a din, but Zach and I managed it with amazing regularity.

What *was* impossible to sleep through was the incessant banging at our door. With great annoyance I forced open one eyelid in a vain attempt to discern the meaning of the angry red blur the loud Thing wished so fervently to bring to my attention.

"Shut up, Thing!" I growled as I flailed and slapped at the snooze button. I wanted nothing more in the world than to give in to the siren song of my pillow, but alas, its peaceful melody was quite drowned out by another barrage of banging at the door and the unsilenced alarm wailing on the other side of the room.

"Zach…" I gazed blearily over at my roommate, who had his pillow and all his covers piled over his head.

"Zach!!" I hollered above the noise that threatened to turn the day rotten before it had even begun.

"Dammit…" I rolled out of bed and stumbled to the far side of the room, grumbling every step of the way. After a number of vivid curses and a few well placed whacks, the other alarm fell silent and, with it, the angry assault upon our door. With a prodigious yawn I stumped over to my trusty coffeepot which sprang to life, chugging its cheery gurgling hiss. It was Sunday, and as much as my eyes rebelled against the sunlight streaming in between the thin curtains, I had to admit it was a beautiful day.

As I sat impatiently awaiting the steaming brew which would transform me from The Morning Beast back to my more agreeable human form, I lit a cigarette and coughed.

"You've gotta quit smoking," I admonished myself, even as I took another drag and stared absently out the window where the Christians of our house prepared to embark on their weekly excursion to commune with their God. I was halfway through my second cup of coffee when Zach finally stirred.

"Mornin'," I said.

The only reply I received was a bearish growl as he disappeared out the door, presumably in search of the tarlike substance that he called "real coffee." I found it greatly amusing that we wound up as roommates and suffered from the same morning affliction.

My musings were interrupted by the distant sounds of hungry goats floating in through the open window, which reminded me that I had chores to do.

"Ah, another day at the ranch," I sighed and got dressed.

"Mornin'," I said again as Zach re-entered the room.

"Hey, man, off to do chores?" he asked.

"Yeah, goats to milk and pigs to slop... What have you got going on today?"

He stood for a moment, his brow wrinkling in deep ponderation.

"I... Well, there was something... Oh yeah, Chuck wanted me to turn on the irrigation down in Asia Field."

"Cool. Want to go swimmin' down at the watershed later?" I asked as I grabbed my battered hat and my stick and headed for the door.

"Sure, why not?... Actually, I think Travis was telling me that there's another watershed down the road from the first one, how 'bout we go check it out?" With a look of despair he fingered his empty pack of cigarettes. "Can I bum a smoke?"

"Indeed on both counts, my friend!" I handed him a cigarette, and as I left, his hacking declaration that he needed to quit smoking struck me as ironically amusing.

The goats at the Guatemala Hillside Barn were hungry and impatient, and they loudly voiced their displeasure at their tardy breakfast.

"Mmmm, corn chops. Enjoy!" I said, as I dumped the feed into their trough. However, as sarcasm is often beyond the grasp of the goat intellect, they made no retort, or perhaps they simply didn't care.

The two pigs heard me coming and immediately launched into a chorus of grunts and squeals and danced a piggish jig. As I dumped the bubbling bucket of slop into the pen, they dove into their trough. They seemed to enjoy having slop dumped on their heads, for it happened without fail every day. I might have found it comical, had I not detested pigs so. As it was, I refused to like them even a little bit. I made the most unfortunate mistake of getting to know the first pig we had when I got to the ranch. When they served him to us for lunch one day, I swore never to befriend another pig ever again. After that rather traumatic incident, I always had to wonder if I was eating someone I knew when I had lunch in the ranch cafeteria.

When I got back to Farside House where Zach and I lived with four other volunteers, Toonces the Cat was the only one home. The Christians, whom I referred to as a collective entity on Sundays, were still off at church doing whatever it is that Christians do. Zach, I presumed, was still off wrestling with the irrigation system.

"Well, cat, looks like it's just you and me." I smiled as I plopped down beside her in the driveway and scratched under her chin. She purred and stretched, and began happily kneading my leg. We lounged in the sun until Zach returned around noon. The cafeteria wasn't serving on Sundays, so we scrounged up a quick lunch and hit the road. Toonces declined to accompany us; I suppose swimming just wasn't her thing.

The sturdy little chevy bounced and rattled its way down the long dirt road that led to the watershed.

"So where exactly are we going again?" I asked my companion at the helm.

"We're going swimmin' aren't we?" Zach replied.

I heaved an exasperated sigh. "No, no, I know that! Where are we going swimming? You said there was another spot."

"Oh! Right," said Zach. "We're going down to the second watershed down the road a'ways from the usual one."

"Did Travis tell you how to get there?"

"Nope… We'll find it."

I laughed, for anytime Zach and I went off exploring we never knew quite where we were going. We just sort of went, and usually wound up somewhere interesting in the process. An hour and three dead end logging roads later, we found ourselves at our destination.

The second watershed wasn't quite the swimming hole I hoped it would be. It was mostly shallow and full of algae and lily pads. There was also a stand of dead trees rising eerily from the water.

"I'm not swimming in that," I stated flatly as we pulled up. I simply cannot deal with swimming in water I can't see in. It gives me the willies.

"Well, let's get out and take a look anyway." Zach shut off his truck and climbed out.

There were a number of rough-looking individuals fishing and guzzling beer down by the boat landing, so we decided that it would be a good idea to explore the shore in the opposite direction.

We saw all manner of birds flittering about and fish darting this way and that between the weeds as we approached. We even saw a raccoon swimming to the far side as we made our way down the makeshift trail and through a barbed wire fence. After wandering for about an hour, we were both hot and tired.

"Did you remember to bring the water?" I asked, sitting down on a log that the beavers had conveniently left behind.

"Uh… I think there's some in the truck, but that doesn't do us much good here, does it?" he replied. He picked up a rock and attempted to skip it across the muck in this swampy section of lake. The rock skipped once and disappeared into a clump of marsh grass, sending a frantic rabbit bounding away as best he could in the muddy terrain.

"You know…" I looked around trying to get my bearings, "If I'm right, the truck is just on the other side of this hill."

Zach gave me a sidelong glance. "Are you sure?" he asked dubiously.

":Nope," I said with a grin, as I started up the steep, tree-strewn slope. Zach groaned and reluctantly followed.

When We reached the top, Zach stopped me, "Hey, check out these strange mounds."

There were several mounds scattered about the woods. They were between shin and knee high and about three to four feet long, with a hollowed out place beside as if dirt had been dug out and piled on top of something.

"Odd," I said, raising an eyebrow. "Kinda reminds me of graves."

"Ya know, maybe this is an old pioneer graveyard or something," said Zach, bending down for closer inspection.

"They're rather small for that aren't they?" I said.

"Well, think about it," said Zach, "if that's what they are, then they've been here a long time. Erosion would have affected them quite a bit, I'd imagine."

"Hmm, very good point." I nodded my agreement. "Shall we

continue?"

With that we resumed our trek. That is until we came across another oddity. We found a ring of trees about ten feet across with an old slanted pine cordoned off by green rope. There were branches piled up en masse between the trees, as if to indicate a rude wall of sorts that had been slumped and broken by time. It appeared to have once been a children's fort.

"Zach," for some reason my skin began to crawl and I felt very uneasy, "I don't like this… I don't quite know why, but there's something…"

"Yeah, I know what you mean."

Neither of us were willing to step into that circle. It seemed almost as if the trees in this place held remembrance of fell deeds. However, I figured I was just allowing my imagination to get the better of me again, and dismissed that train of thought as we prepared to move on.

"Do you see…" Zach began to point.

"That weird multicolored rock?" I asked, for I had seen it at the same moment and was about to ask him that very question.

As we drew closer it became evident that this was no rock, but a pile of clothing half buried by pine needles and decomposing like they'd been there for quite a long time. I poked at the pile with my stick.

"These are children's clothes…" said Zach, an ominous tone in his voice.

Indeed, they were children's clothes… from many different children of both genders. There were even matching outfits.

"Shit…" Something in my head told me to run like hell and don't look back, but I fought my rising panic. Then something beside the pile caught my attention. It was a glove, one of the cheap brown ones, adult sized and bleached out with age. When I turned it over with my stick, the bottom side was stiff and stained a reddish brown hue.

"Um… Zach, does that look like…" I didn't want to say dried blood.

Zach nodded slowly. It seems he didn't want to say it either.

Suddenly the hair stood up on the back of my neck, and I felt as though there were malevolent eyes watching us from behind every tree. I expected some deranged psycho-killer to come screaming out of the woods at any moment, bent on keeping his secret safe.

"Let's get out of here," I said shakily, scanning the trees for any sign of movement.

"Yeah," Zach hastily agreed.

We took off down the hillside, and by a great stroke of luck we burst out of the bushes a scant few yards from the truck. In seconds we were on our way back to the ranch in a great cloud of dust.

The sheriff and two of his deputies arrived at the ranch the next day around noon. Neither Zach nor I wished to return to that place, but we had to be sure. We didn't speak much as we led the way down the twisting dirt road. We were far too preoccupied with our own thoughts for much conversation.

"What if…" Zach didn't finish his statement, but he didn't need to. I knew what he was thinking.

"I don't know," I replied. "God, I hope it's nothing."

"Yeah," Zach nodded gravely, "me too."

We spoke no more until we arrived.

"Now whereabouts was all this?" the sheriff asked, as his deputies unloaded shovels from the back of their truck. I was not at all pleased to note that they had brought enough shovels for us.

"Up the hill, that way." Zach pointed up the steep slope.

With heavy hearts we led the way. We had to slow down more than once to accommodate for the rotund and out of shape officers.

"Now doesn't that make you feel secure," Zach said under his breath, as the sheriff and his men came puffing up the hill. A few yards more and we came, at last, to one of the mounds.

"Yeah, I bet I know what this is," said one of the deputies, "but we'll find out here in a sec."

He took his shovel in hand and prepared to plunge it into the mound. I wasn't sure if I wanted to watch, but I stood transfixed. The moment of truth was upon us.

I almost jumped out of my skin as the shovel tore into the earth with a grizzly, gruesome, bone rending sound. I looked at Zach, who had gone strangely pale and was staring wide-eyed at the mound. Even the stout sheriff was visibly shaken by the noise.

As the shovel rose from the earth, I was sure some child's disembodied head was going to fall to the ground covered in maggots and gore. I almost lost my lunch.

"Yep, that's what I thought," said the deputy, holding a shovel load of pine roots. "Y'see, what happened here was that the wind come along an' blowed over a bunch of pine trees. An' as it rained on them roots with all the dirt, they flattened out to make them mounds, an' the trees rotted away."

After that they made only a cursory examination of the clothes before determining that they were just left by people swimming. They didn't even look at the circle of trees.

Then, patting each other on the back for a job well done, they thanked us for keeping our eyes open and calling them to check it out, even if it was nothing. They drove away, leaving Zach and I to ponder the day's events in silence.

"Did that seem weird to you?" Zach asked me, as we drove back to the ranch. "I mean, why would a bunch of little kids go all the way up the hill to leave their clothes so they could go swimming, and then forget them?"

"Yeah," I said, "but if the cops aren't worried, I'm not going to be either."

"Good point," Zach said, lighting up a cigarette.

Then a most disturbing thought occurred to me: If there were some halfway intelligent homicidal psycho-killer out there, where better to dispose of a load of bodies than in a place with a bunch of mounds that had a perfectly logical explanation?

Either way, that was my last visit to the second watershed. I don't believe I shall return.

Ice Storm

It was my first visit to the woods since the ice storm that wreaked so much havoc and brought Arkansas to a standstill. The remains of trees were twisted and splintered across my customary trails, forcing me to pick my cautious way among their woody corpses. The destruction seemed incongruent with the sun of early spring shining merrily through the budding branches high above. At first, it was hard for me to fathom that mere ice could have caused the scene before me, but then I recalled with startling clarity just how it came to pass…

And on that frigid night when the valley turned to black 'neath the weight of an all encompassing blanket of ice, I discovered just how much comfort a single candle flame in the darkness did not bring.

The Wind howled and raged like a vengeful Windigo from the northern wastes and the night was split all about by the cracking of limbs like gunfire, and tremendous crashes that rang and hissed like the death of a fine crystalline chandelier.

That old familiar fear of the menacing night, that used to send me racing to my mother's arms in the dark hours of the morning as a child, reawakened with a vengeance when the night could no longer be held at bay by the simple flicking of a switch.

Then the sight at the dawning of day, of a world under an enchantment strange and fey—as if all had turned to glass—even the blades of grass were thus entombed, and offered boots no purchase. And making my way to my parents' house—usually such a simple and mundane occurrence—was transformed into a harrowing and perilous adventure of sliding all about and narrowly avoiding gruesome death from above, as towering limbs came crashing at my heels. With an involuntary shiver I came back to myself and my patch of warm sunlight, and sighed a thankful sigh. In time the scars from those bitter nights that the ice waged its slow violence shall fade from the forest, but I for one shall never forget the time when I feared the dark once more.

Girls

It happens time and time again. Whenever I am faced with the prospect of actually talking to a young lady who has captured my interest, I find that my tongue steadfastly refuses to yield intelligent conversation, and that whatever meager wit I might have possessed is nowhere to be found. The world seems to swim before my eyes, a war rages in my innards between a horde of fuzzy kittens and a thousand butterflies, and my knees become possessed of such quaking as to rival the dreaded death wobble of a downhill bike.

At this point, I generally stammer some lame excuse of an extremely important prior engagement only just recalled, and flee without so much as a backward glance to some safe place where none shall see my failure painted in red upon my cheeks and burning ears, and curse myself for a coward and a fool. Each time this occurs, I swear that the next time I won't run, next time I'll conquer my stark driving terror and manage an intelligent conversation; and, if that goes well, I might even conjure the courage to ask her out. Unfortunately, I haven't managed it yet, but next time… yeah, next time.

Before the Dust had Settled, Before the Flag was Trendy

These terrorists who attacked on that fateful Tuesday made some serious miscalculations. I assume they took our diversity for genuine division that would fall upon itself when faced with such a crisis, and I also assume they thought their attack on the supposed icons of America would have some demoralizing effect beyond the travesty of lost lives.

In the first place, America is very much like a rather dysfunctional family. We argue and bicker, hold petty grudges, and many of us really don't like each other even a little bit, but let some outsider step in and mess with any of us and we all turn on them in an instant, and people who would have gotten into a fistfight two seconds before stand shoulder to shoulder to face this threat to our people. That's just what families do, and it's never wise to stick one's nose into their business.

And as for the second, in so diverse a culture, icons really don't matter that much, for everyone has their own view of important things. I know there's people who're enraged that it was the world trade center or the pentagon, but these are buildings most of us have never seen—and thus, beyond a passing knowledge that they existed, they weren't important. They could've just as well blown up a Wal-mart and a Dairy Queen, the effect would be the same. It's not what was attacked that matters, it's the fact that strange people came into our home and killed our family members that's cut us to the bone. And one other thing they failed to understand, terrorism does not plunge us into hysterical fear, it makes us really, really mad.

So I went down
to the used heart dealer,
as mine has seen
better days.
I asked
what I could get
for trade in
on my old one.
The man just laughed
and said I'd get more
for a one-eyed
bow legged duck,
who'd recently
been hit by a
train…

The Captain vs. The Varmint Horde Part VII

And so it was The Captain, my dear ol' dad, stood on the deck in the darkness, between the spotlights that brought a virtual daylight upon the yard. He had been out there every night for a week, in the rain and the cold, in unsleeping vigilance defending his home against a foul invasion of skunks bent on breeding an army in the wall behind Dad's bed. It was almost as if the entire skunk nation had a vendetta against him.

Mother said I should go help him, and in truth I thought she sounded a little worried when she said, "Your father is out there muttering to himself with a gun," though I really didn't see the cause for any alarm, for The Captain had been waging his battle with the varmint horde for years without incident.

I wasn't worried, that is, until I collected my shotgun and joined him in the darkness. He had a rather wild look about him with his hair askew, standing poised, ready, scanning the night for any hint of movement in the shadows, and darting furtive looks behind him. His eyes, hollowed by lack of sleep, held that particular fire of a man driven nearly mad in his obsession, and indeed as I drew near I could hear a soft grumbling of which I only caught snatches of words like, "furry som'bitch" and "motherfucker, I'll kill you."

When I arrived, The Captain assigned me the south quadrant and gave me fervent, detailed instructions on standing watch and scanning back and forth, starting at the deck, along the bushes, the space under the car, out along the edge of the darkness by the woods and back.

"Keep your eyes moving, and keep scanning back and forth, they're sneaky little bastards. They're coming, we'll get 'em, though. They're out there, I can smell 'em! I'm gonna get you little som'bitch, Ooooh yeah, come on… Little furry bastards fuckin' in my walls and blastin' me at three in the morning, ooooh I'm'ona kiiill you. You just scan back and forth, don't let 'em sneak past you!"

I decided it would be wisest just then to simply follow my instructions without question, and there we stood for the next three hours in the cold, Dad admonishing me not to make a sound anytime I shifted my weight, or sniffled from the chill.

Dad suddenly became tense. "Did you hear that?" he said.

I didn't.

"Under the deck… They're under the deck, sneakin' in behind us! Oh, I'm on to you now…" he growled, as he lay prone with his .22 propped on the bottom stair like a sniper, peering into the gloom under the deck along the foundation of the house, which he assured me was one of their well worn trails.

I took his word for it. I was seriously beginning to doubt there were any more skunks left after the four or five he had shot that week, but as he swore there were two more out there—somewhere—I was resigned to my post. The night was silent except for the occasional whispered "motherfucker" and "kill" that came from the direction of Dad. I was leaned heavily upon a pine tree, my mind clouded by thoughts of my bed, when suddenly I saw something in the middle of the yard and headed our way. At first, I couldn't tell what odd manner of creature this was, for it was mostly white and had its neck stretched out long and high to sample the air. As it drew its head back down, I saw it was a skunk—and a big one at that. My first thought was to warn Dad, and I tried to silently get his attention, but so bent he was on catching them sneaking under the deck that he didn't notice. The skunk turned and made as if it were heading to the house, I had no choice. I cocked my shotgun as quietly as I could, brought it smoothly up tight to my shoulder and the world rang loud as the gun bucked and spat a gout of flame. The skunk flipped three times in the air before it crashed and skidded across the ground. I think Dad had forgotten I was even there, for he sprang straight into the air like a cat and whirled around, wide-eyed and shaky. I was shaky, too.

I was annoyed when Dad wouldn't let me shoot it again, it was still twitching as things do, and I'm a firm believer that if it's still twitching it's not dead yet, but he assured me that it was, in fact, quite dead. Then the air was filled with the acrid, burning stink of skunk, a final parting shot by the deceased varmint.

Dad praised my shot, and though I did take a fair amount of pride that I helped him defend the homefront against invasion, I still felt terrible about it. Dad did, too, though it didn't stop him form taunting the corpse.

"Got you, you sombitch! An' I'm gonna get your girlfriend, too, oh don't you worry. One more to go, motherfucker, one more to go…"

I really can't blame him, after all, for he was the one under a ten-year siege by varmints, and really, there's only so much being blasted by skunks in your own bed at three a.m. one can take in the middle of the night before you begin to take it personally.

At that we both went to bed, and though The Captain did stay up late to deal with the last of this particular wave of skunks for the next couple of nights, he wasn't muttering anymore and that crazed gleam did leave his eye, for which Mother and I were very thankful. I wish I could say that was the end of it, but alas, the next time it was armadillos…

Zzzzzzzz....

    I find it odd that in childhood we rebel against sleep for all we're worth, always begging for a bedtime extension, ten more minutes, five more minutes, just one more minute, please? Striving for wakefulness and insisting we weren't sleepy even as our drooping eyelids betrayed utter exhaustion. Then somewhere along the way something shifts—suddenly we can't seem to get to bed soon enough, and it's the morning that finds us begging for ten more minutes, as we beat wailing alarms into submission with half lidded curses and poorly aimed flailings at the snooze button, striving for dreams once more, and insisting we'll get up in just a second and we can still make it on time.

    Perhaps this is our penance for those college years when two hours of sleep would sustain us for three days, of frenzied research papers due at eight a.m. yesterday, and wild parties that raged till ridiculous hours of the morning through the halls of the dorm.

    Whatever the reason for this complete flip of sleep's desire, I may never figure out, but as I'm on the latter side of this issue there's a pillow calling my name, and something tells me it's past my bedtime. So young and old alike, I bid you all good dreamings.

Spring

Springtime is upon us once more, and the world is riotous with green and flowers. The days have grown warm enough to shed our heavy winter raiment and most everyone is reveling in sunshine and blue skies. I say most everyone, for there are those of us who wouldn't mind skipping this season entirely. Love is in the air, you see, and it coats everything in a thin dusting of greenish yellow and plunges us into a hell of sneezing and headaches and allergy pills.

I can't really take anything for my allergies, though, for everything on the market makes me all shaky or dim witted, knocks me out, makes me feel my hair growing, or makes the world look like a slide from an old viewmaster viewer. I'll take sneezing and headaches over that any day. I do wish, of course, that I could enjoy the spring more, for it is indeed so beautiful and refreshing after the bleakness of winter, but most of the time I find myself cursing the trees and wishing they could have evolved some more accurate means of procreation so they wouldn't subject everyone to their windborne tryst. But I suppose having half of yourself stuck in the ground would put a bit of a damper on dating opportunities. So I guess I'll just keep sneezin', and hope that the end is coming quickly.

I really hate lawnmowers
first thing in the morning,
dopplering in and out
of dreams—
Rising to
A wrath inspiring hum,
then fading
into vain hopes that
the bastard's finally done.
But then, damn it all!
Here the som'bitch
comes again!

Poppyseed Smugglers

Somehow in our packing no one noticed that the nine loaves of poppyseed bread (which my family happens to be extremely fond of) all wrapped in foil and stacked in neat little rows in the middle of the large yellow suitcase, appeared to be several kilos of something extremely illicit, and of course I, the most suspicious lookin' of our whole group, happened to be in charge of said suitcase. Somehow I knew that when our turn came to push the button, the customs traffic light, which had blinked green for everyone else, was going to suddenly decide to turn red and I was going to have to explain in my very poor Spanish the concept of poppyseed bread to a bunch of Mexican customs officials who spoke very poor English.

I conveyed my trepidations to Mother, as the line grew steadily shorter. She took my baggage claim ticket, and prying loose the staple, switched numbers with me quick as a flash. It was a good thing she did for, sure enough, the light blinked red and we were directed to place our bags on the inspection table and crack 'em open. Visions of Mexican prison floated through my mind and I was more than a little nervous. Fortunately for us, Mother conveniently forgot to add the yellow suitcase to the pile and nonchalantly passed it behind her for one of the other family members to cart off unnoticed as the customs officers thoroughly poked through my large backpack.

Here's where it gets fun, my grandmother tried to pick it up, but it was too heavy, and she fled the scene, loudly whispering apologies, and left mother hissing and pointing at the suitcase in a way that I feared would definitely draw attention to the fact that we were up to something. I did my best to cause a distraction by purposefully misunderstanding the orders to open my second bag and instead opening more compartments on my backpack. Next came my uncle, heavily laden with scuba gear. After a valiant attempt full of grunts, a loud thump and a grumbling negative informed me he couldn't get it either. I was becoming extremely worried now, for the customs officials, who had, at first, seemed mildly bored, were now beginning to regard us with odd looks and poked a little more closely through my backpack again. Thankfully my cousin Sarah, blessed with an athletic build, cooly hefted the worrisome burden and sauntered right out the door before anyone was the wiser. Just how we managed to pull it off I'm not entirely sure, but next time, I think I'll vote against the trauma of poppyseed bread.

Unwelcome Visitation

It was 2:48 a.m. when the shattering of glass downstairs brought me careening from bed, bleary eyed, wild haired, buck naked and wielding a very large broadsword. I thundered down the stairs, roaring like some vengeful Norse god (that's about the closest thing to "What in the heck is going on down here?" I can manage five seconds into wakefulness and charging into battle). The effect was stunning. The poor little possum just didn't know which way to run and so urinated all over the windowsill, which had until this point been inhabited by some very large wine bottles, the very ones, in fact, that had brought me from my respite when they shattered all over my floor. Just how the little bastard got in I have no idea, but I went and opened up the large sliding glass door to provide an easy escape route and proceeded to scare him out of it.

Only, he didn't cooperate. He took off like a shot across the room and hid behind a large bookshelf. "A- Frame" houses are not conducive to catching small furry animals, for all along the walls there is this convenient runway that's perfectly large enough for them, but too small for you. A large amount of banging, yelling, cursing, and poking with long sticks ensued, as I chased this blasted possum into and out of every conceivable hiding spot two or three times over, resorting at one point to blasting him with water (let me tell you, wet possums smell bad). Finally, I cornered the damn thing behind the bunk beds and managed to grab him by his slimy tail and chuck him out the door. He hit the ground runnin' and I was left sweaty, my house in shambles, and wide awake at 3:26 a.m.

A Moment in a Tale from the Shores of Somewhere Else...

The sunlight filtered through the canopy in soft golden rays. The fair folk flittered and whizzed about, as fair folk tend to do on lazy, sunny days, and the voices of the birds were raised in a chorus of joy. The faerie paused their dance and the birds fell quiet, for there was a something in the air—perhaps it was a sound, or perhaps an impression of a sound from afar, or mayhap just an eerie feeling that something was about to happen. A strange low hum began to emanate from two trees that grew together near the top, forming an unmistakable arch, and the air between them began to shimmer and stir like a heat haze on a beach.

Suddenly there was a *Flash* and from the shimmering gate a figure careened frantically into existence, skidding backward on the leaves as he whirled to face the portal. Just then a number of slimy, claw-covered tentacles swept out of the shimmer to claim him. His walking stick became a spinning blur about him as he laid waste to the tentacles, each one dissolving into an oily foul-smelling smoke only to be replaced by three more. It seemed that he would be overwhelmed at any instant, but he dove aside and slapped his palm upon one of the trees that formed the gate and shouted a Word. Silence fell, and he fell with it...

A groan issued from the young man crumpled upon the ground, and he forced himself into a sitting position.

He was covered in blood, ichor, and worse, ached in a thousand places, and he discovered to his great surprise he was, in fact, still alive.

After a few moments of groans and grumbles, he pulled a small flask out of his pouch, took a sip, and descended into a fit of coughing. He shook his head and his eyes came properly into focus at last. Cautiously and with several more groans and curses he managed to struggle to his feet, and limping over to the gate trees he laid his head against a trunk "Thank you ever so much, tree. Thought I was toast that time." He patted the rough bark and looked around. "Sorry if I caused any alarm," he called to the forest in general, for he could tell it was an enchanted place and knew it was never wise to cause a ruckus in such places without affording the proper respect.

"I do appreciate that no one ate me while I was indisposed." He bowed low to the trees, and pulling a large clear crystal from his pouch he laid it on the ground between the gate trees as an offering to the spirits of the place.

He limped over to where his beaten wide-brimmed hat and his pack had fallen during his fray, and collecting these with some difficulty (more groans and curses), he wondered where he had landed himself this time. Gatecrashing was an imprecise and dangerous art, for there was no telling where one could wind up, and it was only advisable if one were dead meat anyway. He tried to run a hand through his hair, but the usually curly mane was matted with gunk, so with a sigh he limped off in search of a stream or a pond, or some means by which to become clean again, for he hated being slime-covered and funky. He dug a pipe from his pouch and snapped his fingers, producing a small flame just above the tip of his thumb. Puffing his pipe into life he sent sweet-smelling rings drifting through the trees as he limped along and tried not to think of the horrors he had just escaped, or those who fell along the way…

After an hour or so of wandering, he found just what he had been looking for. A stream merrily bubbled along its course through the wood and widened into a shallow pool ringed with ferns and great cypress trees. It certainly seemed a safe enough place to bathe, for there was no hint of danger in the air, but ever since that incident with the vampire carp he was cautious about nice-looking pools in strange lands, so he settled down next to one of the great trees to watch for a bit. He sparked his pipe once more and sang a soft melancholy tune. He knew he was being observed, though whether just by the trees and regular forest denizens he wasn't sure. This place reminded him of home, for he grew up in an enchanted forest, thus he was well at ease despite the predicament of not knowing where in the maelstrom of worlds he might possibly be.

At least he had wound himself up on the happy side of these woods, he mused, as he blew a large smoke ring, for he knew that every enchanted forest had that other side that wasn't at all happy.

He could see the faerie and other such things all over the place, but as it was they all seemed to be going about their own business and taking no more note of him than was usual, and that was a good sign, for such beings always stop and watch if some mischief is about to befall an unwary traveler. They find it terribly amusing.

"Well, I can deal with this funk no longer," he proclaimed, standing up and flinging down his hat, "if anyone is going to be offended at the sight of my lily white ass, I suggest you avert your eyes!" As there were no gasps of shock or giggles forthcoming, he figured it was safe enough and proceeded to peel away his filthy, stiff clothing, wincing as the cloth tore free from his wounds. He piled all his things together at the base of the tree and with a rune-scribed dagger drew a circle in the dirt about them.

"Stay," he said severely, pointing the dagger at the pile. He knew that leaving one's pants unwarded in an enchanted forest was the fastest way to wind up nekkid, darting from tree to tree, chasing down some mischievous little sneakthief (who would inevitably run off to the nearest bramble patch), while the rest of the woods got a good laugh—and that was an indignity he was not going to suffer ever again.

The water was a bit chill, but quite pleasant all-in-all as he eased his aching form into the pool. He wanted nothing more than to plunge headlong underwater, but he knew better. With the tip of his dagger slicing through the water he drew a ring about the circumference of the pool, almost jumping out of his skin when a large bullfrog plopped into the water right next to him. He hastily skirted a hollow log, poking out of the far bank for it gave him the willies and he could feel something in there watching—he just hoped it wasn't anything nasty. When he finished his circle he felt better, though still wary, and he set about the business of becoming clean. He reached over to his pack and rummaged for a stoppered vial of something that looked like white sand, and set to his hair and face. Whatever it was smelled like spring rains and refreshed the spirit as it dispensed with the grime, and soon he was singing a merry wordless tune and splashing about like a four-year-old.

He found that most of the blood caked on his form didn't belong to him, and that, he supposed, was a good thing, though he did have some difficulty prying a barbed fang out of his thigh, and there was a cut on his sword arm that probably needed stitching, but there was nothing for it. He rummaged in his bag for another vial of clear liquid and a packet of leaves. Pulling the cork from the vile he hesitated for a moment, then with a resigned sort of grimace he poured a dash of the liquid into his wound. He did his best to stifle the shriek, but it made the forest go quiet for a moment nonetheless. His arm smoked faintly for a moment as he clutched it, quivering, and blood began to flow freely once more. When he could draw breath again, he unwrapped the packet of leaves and pulled a pinch of amber-hued tree sap from it. He packed it into the gash and stuck one of the leaves firmly into place over the wound.

"Well, that'll leave a nice scar," he sighed. "Now for the leg," he said, almost regretfully. He didn't shriek near as loudly that time.

After that he pulled himself from the water, and dug in his pack for his sarong, a black cloth with white designs, which he wrapped about him like a skirt, and he stood and stretched in the sunlight wringing out his long hair. The faerie did take note at this point, for he was no longer the bedraggled and unfortunate traveler who had limped into their woods—he was something else entirely. He was not a large young man; in fact, he was quite small in stature, no taller than five foot four at best, but his form was like that of an ancient hero sculpted by the gods in perfect miniature. He was also possessed of an odd beauty, like some fey spirit from the wild, with his mane of curls that shined all copper and gold, and laces of silver here and there, and his eyes alive and sparkling with glad mischief. One might think he was elven, or faerie-kin, or a something not quite mortal at any rate, and in truth he was a bit of something, though even he knew not what.

He sighed, and like a cloud that obscures the sun, a slight shadow obscured his shining form and he seemed more like a normal human again, though the watching faerie now knew what he kept hidden.

He returned to his pack and pulled out new clothes (his old ones were beyond repair, and some of the blood stains carried too much sadness to bear them), and clad in a billowing white shirt that laced up the front, some faded blue-jeans, and a pair of black knee high boots that turned down at the top, he fancied he looked like quite the piratical poetical rouge, and finally felt like himself again.

He removed the wards he had placed upon the pool and his pile of stuffs, and sat in a patch of sunlight for some bread, cheese and wine from his pack (anyone paying attention might note that there seemed to be an awful lot of stuff in there for such a small pack, but no one was).

Thus sated, he puffed his pipe into life once again and let his mind drift with the sweet smelling rings up away through the trees into a much needed nap…

My best friend's new neighbor
is a dwarven shield maiden
who may very well
be a prostitute…

Infernal Contraption

I was hot. I was thirsty. All I wanted was a Sprite. The coke machine looked so friendly and inviting when I approached, but soon I was certain that the blasted thing was harboring some malevolent demon. I mean, there was absolutely nothing wrong with my dollar bill. It was genuine US currency, legal tender, but the machine kept spitting it back out at me over and over again. First I tried straightening out the corners, to no avail. Then I flattened it against my thigh just to be sure it wasn't overly creased, but it got three quarters of the way in and came shooting back out again. After checking the diagram to make sure I was going about it the right way and two more failed attempts I began to get annoyed, for I was very hot standing there in the blazing July sun with the object of my quest, my cold tasty beverage, locked in the obstinate machine before me.

I resorted to a desperate trick I learned in junior high back when the dollar bill slots first came out and they tended to be excessively picky about wrinkles and such, I licked the back of my dollar (it tasted really bad and I tried not to think of where it had been before I got it) and rubbed it back and forth on the corner of the coke machine till I was certain it was good and flat. It went all the way in before it decided to spit it out that time. That was it, I'd had enough. And I stomped off into the blazing sun muttering to myself and wondering about the legal ramifications of assault and battery on a coke machine.

Swelter

I remember in the depths of winter, when I had to bundle up under a mountainous pile of blankets, thinking how nice it would be when summer came and I wouldn't have to deal with my toes being cold all night, and it wouldn't be such a trauma to leave the warm haven of my winter nest come morning. Now that it's summer I find I would welcome a bit of that winter chill, for somehow my mind managed to gloss over those little things like how your bed radiates heat after a day of no air-conditioning or just how annoying the rattling of a loose fan cage is, or even that one blasted mosquito that managed to sneak in and spends all night feasting on anything sticking out from under the covers. It seems that whatever season I happen to be in I wish it was some other one, I suppose because it's hard to remember what it's really like to be cold when you're drenched in sweat and even the fan is blowing hot air. Perhaps next winter, when I'm cursing my cold toes and wishing for warm weather, I'll remember what it was like to toss and turn through the dark hours of sweltering midsummer nights, or perhaps I'm simply cursed to be malcontent whatever the weather.

Cheap Orange Juice

Gods, I hate cheap orange juice! The not quite syrupy thickness, combined with an affected sweetness reminiscent of a possum decomposing a'ways upwind on one of those oppressively humid days in July, always makes me grimace as it slides down my tongue to slosh freely about my belly, seemingly of its own accord.

The residue of citric funk that makes my teeth all slick and lingers with a subtle burning in the back of my throat, reminds me of the time I wound up with a whole mouthful of swampmuck (nevermind how I managed that one, but the sensation is most disconcertingly similar).

However, when you're dusty and hot from playing all day and your choices are down to what's in the fridge and tepid tap water, more oft than not you'll opt for the fridge.

Perhaps in a swig or two I'll grow weary of the grumblings of my tummy and cease this wanton assault upon my pallet, because, Gods, I hate cheap orange juice—but at the moment I'm too thirsty to care.

Internal Controversy

I was appalled when I heard that children had brought Death to those halls we all walked, and visited it upon the classmates and teachers we all, in essence, knew. I remembered them from my own schooldays, for the stereotypes are ever the same. You had the royalty—the jocks, the preps, the cheerleaders. There were also those who just don't get messed with—the hoods, the thugs, the cowboys, the gang bangers. There were the Jailors— the teachers, the principal, the coaches. Then you have the quiet ones—the nerds, the dorks, the freaks, the geeks, the weirdos, untouchables, the outcasts. I was one of these.

The abuse we took (for we had no choice but to take it) was almost beyond bearing. We were laughed at, picked on, beat up, the butt of jokes, stuffed into lockers or trashcans, and looked upon with exactly the same expression one wears when they've just stepped in dogshit—and why? Each person who was ever relegated to the bottom of the junior high totem pole has asked this question. The answers were varied, and never good. We suffered this treatment because we were different, or perhaps funny looking, or not smart enough, or too smart for our own good, poor, fat, short, or tall, or sometimes we were just an easy target, something to do because they were bored and found our torment somewhat amusing.

Day after day, year after year, it was borne for so long it became cliche, a joke, just a part of growing up. The teachers knew it was going on—did they do anything about it? Sometimes, if they saw, and even if they did do something, it often made things worse.

Many of the coaches often seemed to encourage it, or even participated at times. And the principal only became involved if one of us had the audacity to forget our place and fight back, then we were in as much trouble as our tormentors. When we made it out, we bore our emotional scars like the lashmarks of a slave. We, all who faced that teenaged hell, are forever marked—even if we adjust later, we remember. Some of us will never fully heal. The pain of the quiet ones, as a whole, lived on in the corridors, festering and growing into a malignant thing, for nothing ever changes there.

Most of me—the logical, mature, grown-up me—was appalled when I heard the news that some kid went nuts and came to school with a bag full of guns, horrified at the teachers and students who died. But there was a part of me, small and secret—the part that bears the scars, that came home in tears, who used words that were too big for so undeveloped a body, who was never cool, never given a chance to be, who was kicked and poked, and fucked with, and laughed at, and teased, and, and, and… That little part raised his head with a wicked gleam in his eye, and with a grim humorless smile he said, "That's what you get. You've had it coming for a long time, motherfucker. We bent over and took it one too many times. You finally pushed us too far. Guess you're not laughing with your little friends now, huh?"

The quiet ones have spoken at last.

Don't fuck with us anymore…

Evening of Seasons

 I used to dislike autumn, for it signaled my return to school, which I hated above all things and was a constant trauma from the first day of kindergarten onward. For years after I finally graduated, the first cool days would send me into nervous fits, with a slight paranoia about being incarcerated once more in a land of crowded halls and tiny desks and subjected to homework—which I generally didn't do; long Division—which I still have nightmares about; and being mercilessly teased for my small stature, large vocabulary, and prodigious imagination—which probably accounts for the introverted streak in my personality.
 Now autumn is my favorite time of year, with its mind-boggling blue skies, crisp breezes, flame-colored trees, and an odd feeling in the air like magic. I feel rather cheated now that I lost so many autumns to the trauma of my schooldays' hell. With the climate such as it is, we're lucky if Arkansas gets two weeks of such weather, for it seems that lately we've pretty much gone from the blaze of summer straight to the frigid, steel grey skies of winter, and the leaves have simply gone from green to dead on the ground. Perhaps this year autumn shall linger for a while, so I might enjoy it at my leisure, for I do so enjoy the evening of seasons.

Bees

One day I was outside in the yard with Dad, and on this particular day he had decided that the ditch beside the road had become too overgrown and needed cutting. And so it was that he set to work hacking away with a swing blade, sending great swaths of honeysuckle and other debris flying through the air. It held my interest for a minute or two, but I soon became bored with what I had decided was grownup stuff, so I turned my attention to playing and shortly forgot all about Dad and his swing blade.

It wasn't long, however, before I noticed that the rhythmic metal-on-weeds sound had been replaced by an odd hum that was growing louder by the second, and Dad was hollering something from the porch. He sounded distressed. "What?" I hollered back.

He was flailing his arms about in the oddest manner as he hollered again, but I still didn't quite catch it over the humming. "What??" I hollered again. I couldn't imagine what this was about.

"BEES!!!" Dad yelled, his face a mural of terrorized frustration, his fists shaking before him for emphasis and, indeed, he was quite correct. The air all about me was swarming with a hoard of flying, stinging, angry-that-their-house-had-lost-its-roof-to-a-vicious-swingblade-attack, Bees.

I ran. Straight through the middle of them I fled, and miraculously passed the gauntlet unscathed. Dad, however, was not so lucky, though to his credit he suffered many of his stings covering my escape (thanks, Dad), and the swelling went down eventually, with the aid of copious amounts of meat tenderizer. Thus was born the ill-fated game of—piss off the bees and run.

Um... Hey, Santa?

And so it is that Christmas eve draws neigh, and I'm not even really excited. No one is, it seems, almost as if all the joy had been sucked from the air, or someone had shot Santa Claus. Perhaps it's all the media hype and high pressure sales pitch that starts up so shortly after Halloween that sucks all the fun out of Christmas. It doesn't help that there's been an uncomfortable unconvincing cheeriness that could turn in an instant to tears, on the Christmases since my grandfather died. I'm sure tomorrow when the family gathers and the songs are sung and such, perhaps then, surrounded by the truth of love and togetherness, I'll finally be able to enjoy the season. It's all just so very stressful this year... Christmas isn't supposed to be stressful, is it?

Traditions

On the night before Christmas we gather our clan up the hill at my grandmother's house. And in the living room, by the light of the odd little tree composed of bare branches snowed white and hung with birds and stars and twinkling lights, we rejoice and remember, and sing the old yule songs (though we sing many da-da-da's and dum-dum-dum's in place of the words we remark every year we need to have written down and passed among us for the occasion). Then comes the tale of this very night, *The Night Before Christmas* is read once again as it has been for as long as I can remember. The night is filled with laughter and cheer, talk of nog filled with grog, and Christmases past, (and usually a disagreement or two on the details of such, and a tense moment of making hoolies behave when it's time to sit still for pictures). Then we sing one more carol or two, then to bed—to our sugarplum dreamings that Santa might pay us a visit.

Upon the next morn we awake to delight, and Christmas morning is filled with the sounds of ripping paper and an air of excitement. After we've had our presents at home, it's back up the hill to Meme's once more, for bloody marys and sausage balls and more presents galore, flashing cameras and hugs and smiles all around. Then we set upon our feast, and eat till we can eat no more (if there is one thing my family can agree upon, it's feasting). And groaning under the weight of our full bellies, we gather our haul and make our way homeward, to play with our toys till night comes upon us again.

With the darkened hours comes one more feast, we all go to T and Captain's house, where cornish hens wait steaming and we pile our plates high with more than we can possibly eat (though we usually do anyway and then some) and we talk and we laugh and love all together. And so the night draws to a close and with it our Christmas ends once again.

Of all the Christmases I've ever heard tell, ours, it seems, is by far the best. So to this family of mine I give all my thanks, for making my Christmases shining and special.

I thank you all for these traditions…

Dork

Perhaps it was sixth grade when we were assigned to write two whole paragraphs on the subject of our favorite role model. At first I pondered which of mine I was going to write about, when I came upon two disturbing discoveries—one, we were going to have to read our paragraphs in front of the class, and two, my idea of a role model drastically differed from those of my classmates.

They buzzed with talk of parents, and sports heroes, movie stars, and other normal-kid role models, and I knew in no uncertain terms that the second Indiana Jones, Luke Skywalker, or Gandalf left my mouth I would instantly open myself to merciless ridicule and mocking for the rest of my adolescent life (eleven-year-olds are unparalleled at that), and I'd suddenly find myself on social par with the smelly kid in the back of the class who ate boogers.

It was one of those moments of clarity that informed me I was profoundly different from my peers, and being already marked by the fact that I was the smallest kid in school and possessed one of the largest vocabularies, I certainly wasn't going to add this piece of ammunition to the pile. I conveniently forgot to write my two paragraphs. Of course I caught flack from the teacher, and from those bossy girls whose homework was always perfect, but at least the secret of my utter dorkdom was still safely kept.

I Hope You Don't Have Issues Now

Seventh grade. Hellish for all, yes indeed. You remember, don't you? The world was circa 1989, and we were all at the height of gawky adolescence.

It was just at the end of sixth period that I unfortunately fell ill, and most unfortunately, Dad was nowhere to be found. He had gone to the bank, they told me, and had to run by UPS, and wouldn't be back to the store for a while. Indeed, I was distraught, for my head started to get this tickle of what would soon become a searing pain, and my poor, poor stomach began to feel a little queasy. Seventh period was social studies, and the teacher, a wild haired batty woman who would drone on and on about whatever social studies was about, grudgingly allowed me to leave class to try to call my dad again twice more, though I don't think she believed I was ill. But alas, Dad still had not returned from his errand. I was becoming truly sick now, and the girls sitting on either side of me kept throwing nervous glances at my oddly greenish white pallor and seemed ready to bolt at the slightest portent of anything icky. So I suffered, huddled in my hard, plastic desk, alternately sweating and shivering, and the teacher, perhaps calloused by years of being stuck in seventh grade, told me to just sit there and I'd be fine. I was far from fine, I assure you. Finally, finally the stupid chime that had replaced bells in the new middle school dinged its pathetic little ding, and wondering where in the world my father was when I was in such a terrible state, I rose from my desk.

As I stood erect, I gained a whole new awareness of my stomach and the contents thereof. I was going to vomit. Soon. Though in that moment, through supreme effort of will I managed to get a hold on the maelstrom brewing in my gullet, for I was not going to suffer the embarrassment of a chorused Eeeeewwwwww! punctuated by the sickly splattering sound of puke hitting vinyl tile.

I walked, not ran, for running was more than I could handle just then. I walked down the as yet unfamiliar halls mentally plotting the course to the bathroom, while steadfastly not thinking about what I was about to experience. I remember some people speaking to me, but I marched steadfastly onward without a word, I wasn't opening my mouth for love nor money. It was the dam that held back a grim chunky tide—one tiny crack and it would all be over. I wound my way through the after school throng as deftly as I could, single minded in my purpose—to the bathroom. It was coming, but I held fast.

I rounded the final corner. The bathroom was in sight, not thirty steps away. I remember the strange dim hall, all shades of brown and tan, lined with lockers, and the bathroom door reflecting the recessed track light which shown like a beacon from heaven. I remember the rush of relief as I neared my safe harbor through a surreal haze of barely contained nausea. Then it really was coming. My stomach gave a little twitch that signaled the beginning of the end. It was now or never, I made the bolt for the door—so close, so close.

I was going to make it, it was going to be fine, I wasn't going to be "that little kid who puked in the hall." And unfortunately, Scott, in his usual jovial manner, chose just that moment to say, "Hey, Ryan," and gave me a companionable slap on the back.

It was as if he had hit some firing mechanism, and my world

became one great heave.

I was amazed to see the contents of my stomach launch rocket-like before me, astounded at the cohesive velocity of this gruesome bolt which my gullet had sent forth.

I saw her turn at the sound as she knelt beside her open locker six feet away. I saw her eyes widen to pools of horror as she espied her doom bearing down upon her, heard her gasp and saw her jaw drop open with the realization that there was no escape.

I saw it slam into her shoulder, and heard the sickly splattering sound as two feet of vomit ploughed unerringly to the mark. I remember wishing she hadn't opened her mouth.

All of this in the time it took to bolt past. I had no time for an apology, for I wasn't finished yet. I burst through the bathroom door, and the urinal was as far as I got. The call for a janitor in the west corridor came quickly, and truly I felt terrible, as I finished heaving up my guts, that he was going to have to clean up all this mess, but that was nothing compared to the shame of having puked on some poor innocent girl. I have no idea who she was, no way to say how very sorry I am, but then, nothing quite makes up for being puked on in seventh grade. So, if you ever read this, please know that I didn't do it on purpose, and to this day, fifteen years later, I still feel awful about it. I just hope you don't have issues now...

Reminder

There's a chapstick lip print on the passenger window of my car, left there by the last girl I dated, as a cutesy sort of reminder. Most of the time I forget it's there, or try to at any rate, for we had a falling out that was rather unpleasant in the end. But every so often I notice it again, and experience a nasty pang, for the reminder has lost its cutesy demeanor and turned bittersweet. Every time I see it, memories of *what was* leap up to smack me in the head (which can be rather traumatic when trying to deal with driving) Even after I've hidden away all her pictures, and taken off her ring, and moved my mind on to more productive matters, I still can't bring myself to be rid of that dang lip print. It's silly of me I know, I don't even want to talk to the girl anymore, but still it remains like an annoying song that gets stuck in your head for weeks on end. Perhaps I don't really want to forget, perhaps I look on that lip print and wish that she was still sitting there grinning at me in that shy sort of way she had (even though I know it's far better that she isn't), or perhaps I leave it there as a warning, or a talisman to protect me from the errant stupidity that got me into such a mess in the first place, or perhaps (and most likely) I'm just too darn lazy to go about procuring some Windex.

Sveldon's Date

Sveldon plunged his great shaggy head into the fresh barrel of water. Usually the twigs and leaves tangled in his wild mane didn't bother him, they provided good camouflage for a warrior creeping through the bush and the leavings of previous meals hiding in his beard could come in mightily handy if one were off somewhere and needed a snack. But tonight he had a date.

He shook his dripping locks, throwing great torrents of water all over the place, and grinned at his reflection in his freshly polished breastplate hanging on the wall. Aside from a dent or two, it made a perfectly serviceable mirror. A warrior on the go must often improvise, and besides, mirrors always seem to wind up getting smashed over people's heads after a long night at the mead hall.

Merrily humming the "Ballad of Loki's Lost Love and The One He Found After, It Wasn't a Goat, He Was Drunk," (a very popular tune in those days, unfortunately Loki was not at all pleased to hear that such a disparaging and obviously not true thing was being sung in every mead hall in the land. Finally he decided to just sneak in to all the mead halls after everyone had passed out and steal the wretched song from their minds as they snored away in a mead-soaked fog. Fortunately for us he forgot to steal the title, so we know what Sveldon was humming). Sveldon set to his beard with his fishbone comb yanking out brambles and mats en masse. It took quite some time to tame the wilderness erupting from his chin, but soon enough he was satisfied and turned his attention to the great shaggy mane that crowned his seven foot bulk. Soon the floor was littered with leaves and twigs, some helmet shards from that battle yesterday, and a chipmunk, that had been lost for only Odin knew how long, that was quite pleased to be free of its hairy bondage, and scampered out the door.

Sveldon grinned at himself in his breastplate again, he was so happy he was just about to burst. An actual date, with the girl of his dreams! He sighed and gazed dreamily into nothing, enraptured by visions of feasting with her by his side, throwing bones over each other's shoulders, being partners in the two-headed giant game, and perhaps (he blushed at this) sharing a mead horn later, just the two of them... But Sveldon had no time for dreaming, the sun was fast setting and he didn't want to be late, so he braided wild beard into two great braids and bound his hair behind him with his polished bone hair tie.

The real trauma came when it was time to get dressed. He had positively no idea what he should wear. Should it be the shiny armor or the bearskin shirt? Or maybe just a simple fur trimmed jerkin would do... He fretted and pondered holding up first one and then the other beneath his chin, turning this way and that before his makeshift mirror. Finally he decided on a homespun shirt and his wolf skin vest, and a Kilt he'd picked up on a raid somewhere. He decided against his horned helm, as he thought it might give the wrong impression, he was a gentlemanly Viking after all.

One last once-over in the breastplate, and Sveldon was out the door. Only seconds had passed before he burst through the door again frantically searching for the bouquet of flowers he had picked that afternoon, and a few seconds later found him back again searching for something to put them in. Weapons, clothing, bones, and trinkets flew around the room as he rummaged for anything that would serve as a proper vase. He picked up a wolf's skull and pondered it for a moment, his great brow furring with thoughts of how to make it work. Then Odin shined down upon him inspiration. Sveldon beamed as he stuffed the bouquet into the jaws of the skull, bound them shut with a strip of leather, and set the skull looking skyward upon the table. "Perfect!" he exclaimed, snatching up the flowers as he dashed out the door and leaped astride his giant horse in a single bound. He galloped off into the setting sun, face set in a dopey grin, and that misty eyed look of a Viking in love.

Morning Coffee.
Mumble, grumble, to the shrine
Listen till the fill sounds right
Bleary eye the line for certain
Pour the water
Dump the grounds
Fumble for the filter
Level measure from trembling hand
Flick the switch to life again
Wait, wait, gurgle-hiss
Gurgle-hiss and chug
It sighs.
Stump forward, hallowed cup in hand
Take up the sacred silver spoon
The cream shall be one and the sugars two
To temper it smooth and sweet
Scent the steam and take a sip
Smile to the morning a sigh of thanks.
Amen.

When Guinea Pigs Fly

There were wondrous advantages to living at a summer camp all my life. I got to meet lots of neat people, hang out with the counselors, do what the other kids couldn't and the like. There was, however, one drawback. I was the closest thing to a camper who happened to be around all the time. This meant anytime Dad had one of his hair-brained adventure ideas, I got to safety test it so as to be certain it wouldn't cause injury to a camper and wind up getting us sued.

On one such occasion, Dad decided that a swing was in order. An ordinary swing you ask? My dad? No, not The Captain. It was going to be the swing to end all swings! With a sphincter factor of at least twelve, this swing was designed to make your life flash before your eyes (or at least make you need to change your britches). So, Dad went about making this swing of terror the latest addition to the adventures group (and almost succeeded in plunging to his death trying to tie the rope.) The swing consisted of a very long nylon fire hose, a burlap bag, sawdust, a plastic bag, more sawdust, and in the center, a rock . It was an awesome sight to see the bag rush toward the tree then continue out over the lake, then come swinging back again. After finding the right takeoff angle, Dad decided that the swing was ready to be tested with someone on it, so it was that he called upon me, his trusty son, to serve as his "Assistant"—though a more accurate term would have been "Guinea Pig," and he bade me hop up onto the bag. Being somewhat small in stature, considerably less than four feet tall, it took the aid of my dad to clamber up onto the swing.

"Are you sure this thing will hold?" I asked dubiously, bouncing slightly to test the rope.

"Sure! That rope pulled a bus once, there should be no problem," said Dad cheerfully.

Wouldn't pulling a bus substantially reduce the structural integrity of a rope? I thought, as dear ol' Dad threw out a scoop of catfish food. I didn't voice my concerns for he was, after all, my dad, and he wouldn't put me in any actual danger... Would he?

He took hold of my knees and prepared for liftoff.

"If you fall off, make sure to aim for the water... And watch out for the catfish," he said, digging his feet in for better traction. (I was slightly afraid of the catfish, some of them were large enough to take off my leg, and I wasn't at all certain that they wouldn't do it either.)

With a Tarzan yell Dad pushed me at a run, and then threw me as hard as he could. My momentum carried me to a height of at least twenty feet above the ground, there was a heart stopping moment of a disconcerting weightlessness before my decent, and then I rushed toward the hard-looking tree. That's when I screamed. I thought it was fortunate that I missed the tree until I sailed out over the lake. I looked down and saw the dreaded catfish, for the way they were circling they may as well have been great white sharks. They seemed to be waiting for a tender morsel such as myself to drop into their midst. I screamed again. My testicles drew up into my throat, my stomach had been left somewhere near the tree, and my bladder was on the verge of letting go; it was closely akin to a near-death experience. The adrenalin rush of terrorized excitement was like nothing I'd ever experienced before. It felt like I was flying.

When Dad stopped me and was finally able to pry my fear driven hands from the rope, he knew that he had created the ultimate swing.

Countless children through the years experienced the might of the Great Swing, but none achieved the wondrous terror of the Guinea Pig that flew.

Running The Gauntlet

The sky was overcast as we strode into the sea bearing our masks and fins. The rumbling surf hissed and foamed about our knees and pulled at our legs, and I was certain that at any moment a jellyfish was going to entwine itself about my bare ankles.

"Are you sure you don't want to wear your mother's dive skin?" Dad asked, zipping up his own black and red dive suit. "Those jellyfish are nasty out there."

I pondered it for a moment, as I was clad in nothing more than a speedo and a dive knife, I was probably going to get stung to a fare-thee-well but my pride simply cannot bear wearing neon pink, so I refused, and we continued into the sea.

Once we were chest deep, we donned our masks and fins floating just below the surface so as not to fill our fins with sand. It took years of practice to perfect this little maneuver, and I wondered how we ever managed in Jamaica so long ago with our little orange masks, no fins, and me riding on Dad's back for hours. Once I had gotten all the hair out of my mask I looked around for Dad, and he was frantically pointing behind me. I whirled and found myself face to face with three particularly nasty-looking jellyfish and back-paddled as quickly as I could. Our adventure, it seemed, had begun. Dad struck out toward deeper water, and I followed along beside, swimming an erratic path to avoid the seemingly large numbers of jellyfish pulsing themselves along and trailing their long tentacles. I was wary of course, for I was mostly bare and I didn't fancy getting stung, but it wasn't much of a problem as Dad had assured me that their numbers thinned out farther from shore. What I didn't realize, though, was that what I thought was a daunting number of jellyfish were merely a hint, a vague impression of the hoard we were to encounter, and encounter them we did. Suddenly we were in the midst of a pulsing, heaving wall of jellyfish, from the sand of the sea floor eight feet below to the surface where the surging waves met the sky. I looked at Dad and I could tell by his expression he hadn't quite expected this. He pointed to the waiting gauntlet, and then made a questioning sign. We had been at this for enough years so that I knew exactly what he meant. What he said was, "Would you look at that? Holy shit! Are you sure you wanna keep going, you're pretty bare you know?"

If I had been by myself, I would have turned tail back to the beach post haste, but somehow being in a whole sea full of jellyfish and wearing only a speedo just doesn't frighten me much when Dad is there. I suppose after all my odd adventures with The Captain, I'll follow him anywhere, and I couldn't very well let him go off on this one alone. So with a look of grim determination, firmly convinced that I was toast, I strove forward at full speed and met the terrible tentacled wall head on.

I dodged and dipped and shot through holes that would appear miraculously before my eyes, I plunged with reckless speed through a bizarre tunnel of doom that threatened to engulf me at any second, and I hoped that Dad was faring as well as I, for I had no chance to look though I was aware he was just behind and to the right of me. How far we fought our way ere we were through I can't tell, but suddenly we had done it. It wasn't that there were fewer jellyfish, for there were still multitudes beyond counting , but they were spread out over a depth of thirty feet rather than eight, and it was infinitely preferable. We paused to rest after our harrowing swim, and that's when it occurred to me that we were in deep, man-eating-shark infested waters, for there had been several attacks within a few miles of where we were. Again, had I been by myself I would have fled in terror, but Dad, as always, was still right there, and I knew if a shark showed up that we'd handle it somehow or another, though I did draw my knife just in case.

We swam along the surface for a while, for there were fewer jellyfish to dodge there, and rode the large comforting swells pointing out fish here and there and the large purple sand dollars on the bottom. Dad dove, weaving his way around pods of jellyfish all the way to the bottom, and then weaving his way back up again with a brilliant white sand dollar clutched in his hand. So, it was treasure we were after! Soon we were both diving and weaving for sand dollars thirty feet below. I discovered, though, that it was not so easy as Dad had made it seem. It was a trick that required cunning and patience, and good lung capacity.

I was fine going down, and equalizing the pressure in my ears is something I have a knack for so I didn't have to pause except to avoid waving tentacles and clear pulsing blobs. Once I had acquired my first sand dollar, though, I discovered that thirty feet was a long way down. I was rapidly running out of air, and the route through the jellyfish swarm I had taken down had disappeared, forcing me to find another one. Dad, of course, was swimming around in his languid graceful way, quite serene and unconcerned, and suddenly it clicked. I finally got what he had told me about swimming and underwater and relaxing. So I let go of my rising panic, and, imitating his slow natural rhythm, made my way to the surface before the stars started swimming in my vision from lack of air. After that, the only problem was how to carry all my treasure, for speedos do not come equipped with pockets, and with man-eating sharks in the area there was no way in hell I was going to put up my knife just to hold onto a bunch of sand dollars, so I wound up stuffing them into my suit. Dad was fortunate in that respect, for he could stuff them up his sleeve or down his collar, and mine, well mine came to rest in a much more uncomfortable place. People usually don't consider sand dollars to be spiky sort of things—let me assure you, they are.

After a couple of hours, we were getting prune-ish and chilly, and my speedo could contain no more sand dollars, so we made our way back to shore.

In the quiet, serene depths, I had put the seething, writhing, stinging wall of gelatinous flesh out of my mind, but we were soon in the thick of it again and I found that plunging with the waves was a far different matter than the other way around. Fortunately, by some luck or magick, I managed once again to strive and dodge and dip and whirl my way at harried speed, aided by the water's momentum, even faster than before, through impossible holes and tunnels, and sometimes blind when a wave would crash bubbles all around me, but somehow we made it through to pull ourselves salty and dripping and rubber teethed back onto the beach to divest ourselves of our treasure and our tale of grand adventure. And somehow, speedo clad though I was, I didn't acquire a single sting, and I'm certain I couldn't have pulled that one off with anyone other than Dad by my side. So for the greatest adventures of my life, and the best tales—thanks, Dad.

Timberlake Nights

It's funny how sounds and smells play such a vivid role in memory. Last evening I stepped out on my deck and was met by the rhythmic summer chant of crickets, peepers, and bullfrogs, and the smell of the lake and trees and darkness. For a moment I was a kid again, sitting on the porch of one of the cabins telling ghost stories of The Hermit to the campers, hoping that our counselor wouldn't show up and tell us to get back to bed. And looking forward to the next day of horseback rides, adventures, skits, dances, and clandestine meetings with cute girls on shadowed swings. I could almost hear the hum of the many fans in the cabin windows, and see the night lights that hung from the porches of the cabins.

For that moment I almost believed that when the morning came the cafeteria bell would ring loud and the still morning air would be filled with the sounds of children once more, as it was in the deceptively endless summers of my youth. With a heavy sigh I came back to myself. Save for the nature sounds, Timberlake is quiet now, and the cabins all dark, and their stout stairs that echoed loud even when you tried to sneak are crumbling to dust. These memories made me smile even as my vision blurred with tears, and as I grow older and my younger days fade in my memory, I trust that the summer sounds and smells of this place shall always conjure up what I've forgotten and Camp Timberlake, as it once was, shall never fade away.

He Sighed With a Contented Smile and Shook His Dripping Locks

I stood upon my deck as the wind began to blow. Fierce gales howling from the east set the trees to roaring and veiled the land in dust of long baked earth. Rain was coming.

I raised my arms to the heavens with a broad grin and laughed as the first giant drops plummeted from the heavy clouds, and danced merry circles as the deluge ensued, banishing the dreaded heat that had the land long held in oppressive thrall.

I squeezed tight my eyes against the stinging drops and breathed in the cool scent of rain, and shed my sodden raiment to lie in naked mirth beneath the cleansing rain. The chill of wind on rain-soaked flesh brought rejuvenation to my spirit and cleared my mind of weary thoughts, and the magick of the moment coursed through my blood and set my soul to long forgotten ease.

Then, as swiftly as it had come, the rain rolled on, and the cheery sun shone on a land of rainbowed sparkles and green. I stood once more and faced the sun, and reveled in the soft golden warmth as it caressed my dripping form to dryness. Then, with a contented sigh and a grin, I gathered my very wet clothes and left the world to the sun and the birds as I went back inside the house…

Bonk

They carefully slid and picked their way down the steep shale cliff beside the river and made their way out onto the long promontory of tumbled rock—presumably created to stave off erosion of the banks. One of these young men was a Wizard and the other a Magi—they were something to that effect anyway, or perhaps they were both merely delusioned madmen—whatever the case they were on their usual errand of magickal mischief and engaged in their usual conversation—an unceasing tangle of bizarre and random tangents which somehow managed to yield frequent sparks of enlightenment through the machinations of their conversational magick.

They sat in the shade of the cottonwood trees, spared from the harsh glare of the afternoon sun, watching the river writhe and boil with unseen strife beneath the rolling surface.

The Wizard tossed a rock into the midst of a strange smooth swirl that emerged forcefully from the choppy waves, and it disappeared with an unnaturally loud and oddly hollow and ominous sounding *gloonk*!

"You just bonked a sleeping river demon on the head!" exclaimed the Magi, "I'll bet that just woke him up."

"I'll bet he'll be pissed," said the Wizard, looking worried, "of course, fast as this current's flowing, he'll be a'ways downstream before he recovers sufficiently to do anything about it, I mean it takes a while to figure out what's goin' on when you're sleepin' and get bonked on the head with a big rock."

With that, the Magi seized a rock and hucked it square in the middle of a particularly large swirling boil. *Gloonk*! The Wizard giggled so hard he almost fell off his rock.

"Some poor riverboat crew is gonna catch hell for this you know," said the Wizard, tossing another stone.

"Or some old redneck out fishin' with his buddies," replied the Magi, and they both got a good laugh out of that one.

So there they resumed their conversation, and for the better part of an hour they had a glorious time bonking the river demons on the head to awaken them from their centuries-old sleep. Of course they didn't hit all of them; when they missed, the tell-tale hollow *Gloonk*! was more of the *Splat* one would usually expect from tossing stones in a river, but far more than a few river demons, sore headed and extremely annoyed, went tumbling downstream through the currents that day.

They decided that it would be best to leave their game; however, when the Wizard seized a particularly large rock and hurled it into a particularly large boil, not only was there a *Gloonk*! but also a *Thok*! And a deep *Grumble*! And visions of a demented plesiosaur with overlarge fangs and tentacles suddenly leaped into their heads, and it occurred to them that they were terribly exposed to attack where they sat and their escape route was none too easily navigated at full speed. So they made their cautious way back to the cliff (rather faster than they had come) and scrambled back up among the slick shale and tree roots. They stood for a moment gazing at the river below, and laughed again at the thought of the mischief they had wrought. Then they made their way back to the car, speaking of great magicks, and debating the proper way to enchant a spear…

Exit Stage Left

    And standing upon the stage alone, as the laughter faded beyond the theater door, he smiled a self-deprecating smile. He pulled from one of the pouches hidden beneath his cloak a long stemmed pipe, and worn leather bag of sweet tobacco, and in a quiet voice that nonetheless echoed in the empty cavernous hall he spoke.
    "What if…" He paused for a moment to untie his bag and began to pack his pipe with care. "What if I really did go about my daily life talking to spirits and faerie, and foiling the plans of evil sorcerers, finding Adventure and Magick and the secret things of the world?"
    He drew from his pocket a lighter that he had forgotten was not, in fact, in his pocket at all, a lighter that until he reached for it, lay upon his bedside table at home. He took a moment to puff his pipe into life, the smoke drifting in thick, sweet-smelling rings about the lights hanging high above.
    "What if I really had found a way to catch Dreams by the tail and drag them back to the waking world, or went about releasing Dragons from their age-old sleep in their halls of stone? What If I actually were a seeker of the Mystery as it was in the time of once upon, and had discovered that the truth of Magick was ever so much more astounding than anyone had ever dared to dream…"
    He looked out over the empty rows of seats and laughed softly to himself.
    "Perhaps I am mad, but then perhaps it doesn't matter so long as there is someone to believe that there's more to the world than what meets the mortal eye. Indeed, I say I'm a wizard, an

adventurer, a bard, a something from some other time, some other place, a spirit both fierce and fey, and a servant of that secret which is whispered in the silence. *What if I really am?*"

He raised an eyebrow and puffed thoughtfully upon his pipe again, and was quiet for a long moment, apparently lost in thought.

"The only people who can bring themselves to actually consider that question, are those who know me on sight and thus the question becomes irrelevant. Of course, it does call into question their own grasp of reality…" He grinned an odd grin. "But who's to say what's real anyway?"

With that, he stuffed his pipe back into his pouch and exited stage right, the heavy hollow thump of his boots echoing out across the deserted rows.

There was the loud click of a circuit breaker being thrown, and the lights above the stage cut abruptly, their filaments glowing briefly a deep orange before they faded to black. His boots thumped slowly across the stage once more. He paused in the dim light, spilling through the open back door to draw his cloak more tightly about him, and he peered out both ways to assure himself there was no demon horde laying in wait to fall upon him in the alleyway, then taking up his walking stick he strode out into the world closing the door behind him, leaving the theater to the spirits that always inhabit such places, and thick, velvety darkness vaguely scented of pipe smoke…

Printed in the United States
24706LVS00005B/124-225